familiar kiss

Sherry D. Lewis

Sherry D. Lewis

Printed in the United States of America.
ISBN: 978-0-578-69894-6
First Printing, 2020
Shreveport, LA 71109

Dedication

This book is a dedication to my loving mother, Ethel Mae Lewis-Moore - the person who showed me how to work hard and believe in myself. I would like to thank God and my Savior Jesus Christ for blessing me and for allowing me to share my passion and gift with the world.

I would like to give thanks to my entire family for always being supportive and showing love. This book is also dedicated to my father, Leroy Lewis, II, and to my brothers Shaymon L, Leroy L. III, Jeremiah L., and Gabriel L.

Last but not least, I dedicate this book to the two most important people in my life, Decora L. and Jecory M. and to someone who I'm very thankful for having in my life, Antonio D. H. Thanks for always motivating me to never give up on my goals and for always speaking the truth to me.

Sherry D. Lewis

Part One:

Love at First Sight

Prologue

Have you ever experienced love at first sight? I'm talking about genuine true love. A feeling that was so undeniable that you knew it was meant to be. It seemed so magical that everything just stood still. It's like nothing else mattered at that moment except you and that one person you were destined to be with. Well, I'm about to tell you a story about how it happened for two people.

It took one second for a beautiful woman named Secrets to realize which man she was meant to be with even though some things would occur that would make her think otherwise. However, it was harder to convince the handsome man Distance that they were meant to be together no matter what was right in front of him. Nothing would make him believe it until he finally let in the one thing that he wanted all along - true love.

It all began many years ago during the winter season. It was strange but unique, magical, and crazy all at the same time. Secrets and Distance lived miles apart, but they faced similar relationship issues with other people. She was having problems with her boyfriend at the time and wanted out. The relationship was going nowhere, and she was over it. Distance and his girlfriend had broken up also because they constantly argued. They both wanted different things out of life, and Distance was done. Unbeknownst to the future lovers, Secrets and Distance would eventually meet and experience a ride of romance and drama that they would never forget as they would treasure it forever.

Chapter One

Secrets met Carrion while working at a local restaurant. He really wasn't her type, but he had great conversation. Besides, she was newly single again and wasn't looking for anything serious. As much as Carrion tried to capture her interest, in her heart she knew it wasn't going to last because it just wasn't what she wanted. While Carrion wooed her daily, Rhythm, her ex, constantly tried to win her back. Secrets would always tell him that she didn't want to be with him, but he just wouldn't let go. He realized that he was losing a good thing, but it was just too late. She was gone and would never go back to him.

Secrets finally gave in to Carrion and dated him until he showed his real personality. He was controlling and would lie about everything and would often lose his temper. She didn't even get upset because she didn't plan to stay with him anyway. However, she did begin to like him and was willing to see where it would go. Nevertheless, he proved that he was unworthy of being in her life when he started to lie and blatantly see other women in her presence. Meanwhile, Rhythm continued his pursuit in hopes to win her back. One day he asked if she was dating someone. He even mentioned that it might be someone at her job, but he wasn't quite sure who it could be. Although he'd guessed right, she didn't want any drama where she worked - or any drama period - so Secrets made up a name and said she was dating a guy named Distance. She wasn't about to tell him Carrion's real name.

When Rhythm asked more questions about her new love, she described him as a tall muscular guy that wore glasses and a low haircut. She gave him a completely different description from what Carrion looked like to avoid confusion. Rhythm didn't really believe it.

He told her, "I know that can't be true because I never see anybody by that name or that fits that description at your job."

"Distance quit, and he works somewhere else," she replied.

Rhythm just said, "Whatever," and gave up on trying to figure out who she was actually dating.

She didn't owe anyone an explanation about her love life. She didn't want to lie either, but she did what she had to do. As weeks went by, Secrets began to seek employment elsewhere. The restaurant job was only temporary for her, and she didn't plan to work there long-term. So, she found a better job and left the restaurant business. As time progressed, things started to get very interesting for her love life. She started her new job with no expectations of meeting anyone. All she wanted to do was work, make her money, and go home. She wasn't looking for a love interest. There was no need this time because love came looking for her.

Little did Secrets know she was about to meet a man that would just make her melt. It was love at first sight, and her new lover immediately made her so nervous. She was terrified of falling head over heels for him. It was just something she'd never experienced in her life. She wanted to believe it but didn't think it could happen to her. She had been through so many lies with men, she just didn't want to give love another chance to hurt her.

Secrets focused every day on her daily duties at work. Some guys would have to come to her work area for assistance every day. They needed special assigned keys to perform their daily work tasks. It was her job to sign those keys out to them. One of the guys would always joke and flirt with her. He'd often try to spark conversation to make her notice him. However, she wouldn't give him the time of day. Her mind was set on guarding her heart against any distractions or pain that love might bring. Other ladies that she worked around always loved having his attention, but Secrets could care less. She was just there to do her job.

A few months went by, and fate had to step into her life. She wasn't paying any attention to her knight in shining armor standing right before her eyes. Still, she needed to be reminded that true love was real, and it was staring her right in the face. One day, while she worked really hard on her everyday duties, the equipment she used daily failed. The same guy that would always flirt with her had to come to her work area to assist with the problem. As he began to work on the broken machine, a mutual friend sparked a conversation with him.

Secrets interrupted the conversation. "Girl, you're always talking to someone. Will you let this man finish working on this machine, please? You're distracting him," she joked.

Her friend introduced them to each other as if they hadn't already met.

"Distance, have you met my friend Secrets?"

He just smiled and didn't say anything at first, so the friend continued.

"Secrets, this is my homeboy Distance."

Now, remember back when Secrets was dating Carrion, she pretended that his name was Distance to keep her ex Rhythm from knowing who she was actually dating. Well, here it is. She had spoken this man into existence without even knowing. The exact same name she had made up months ago, wasn't even a thought in her head when she began her new job. What she did notice is when she looked up at him and made eye contact, she experienced something she will never forget. It was like something came over her and she heard these exact words: *"That's your husband."*

She wasn't even looking for a boyfriend - and most definitely not a husband. However, it was like magic sparked between them at that moment. She experienced a different feeling of love like they had known each other all their lives. It felt like they were two people who were lost, and their souls had finally found each other again. Immediately, she was speechless and terrified because she couldn't believe what had just happened.

Distance replied, "Yeah! "I know who she is; I've seen her many times. I would speak to her and try to make conversation, but she would just ignore me."

Secrets replied, "I don't remember you."

Distance told her, "You don't remember my face because you would never look up at me. You would just brush me off and never look my way."

As they continued their

conversation, she soon realized who he was.

"Oh okay! You're the guy that would always be talking and joking."

Distance didn't say anything. He just sat there with a smile on his face. Secrets laughed at the thought that this guy recognized her all along. He was being nice from the beginning, and she just never took the time to look his way. They both exchanged numbers and started to talk to each other outside of work. This was the beginning of an unexpected future.

Chapter
Two

As time passed, things got more interesting in Secret's life. One day Rhythm popped up at her job unannounced to speak with her. Rather than turn him away, she decided to be civil since they had a child together. She went outside to see what he wanted. While they were talking, Distance coincidentally appeared nearby. Without much thought, he yelled to Secrets.

"Have a good day! See you tomorrow."

Rhythm was sitting in his car and brought it to her attention. He obviously never forgot about what Secrets said months ago.

Rhythm asked, "Is that dude's name Distance?"

She said, "Yeah. How do you know him?"

He said, "We went to school together."

She simply replied, "Oh okay," but Rhythm wasn't done with the topic.

"Wait a minute. It sure looks like that's the same description you gave back when you were working at the restaurant. The person you were supposed to be dating was a tall big guy, muscular built with dark skin, and glasses."

She thought to herself that she couldn't believe that she had described her current special friend before she even met him. She recalled telling her ex that the guy had gone to another job back when she was at the restaurant.

"No!" she replied. "That isn't the guy I was talking about back then. Maybe it's just a coincidence, but that isn't him."

"Nah, that got to be him," Rhythm replied as he glanced in Distance's directions once more for confirmation.

"Look, what difference does it make? It's over between us anyway. Besides, that was then, and this is now. All you and I have is our child together. So just focus on that and get out of my business."

Rhythm eventually dropped the subject, and they never had any more issues. Still, she couldn't believe that the guy she made up months ago was actually a real man that she would eventually meet and experience love at first sight coupled with real unconditional love. They also seemed to share telepathy. It was like any time she would mention his name at work, he would walk by. It didn't matter the time of day; he would always appear. It happened so much that it started to freak her out. She would get butterflies each time she laid eyes on him. She would get so nervous that she would lose all her thoughts and just be lost for words.

The more Secrets interacted with Distance, the more she started to see that he was a laidback trustworthy guy. That allowed her to open up to him more. Their relationship progressed, and he invited her to his mom's house, where she met his family. She introduced him to her family as well. They both still lived at their parent's houses. They'd each had their own places before, but sometimes life happens and forces you to move back home. Nevertheless, both families were pleased to meet each of them accordingly.

They continued to date. Distance called her one night to invite her over his friend's house. Secrets was excited to see him, so she agreed to meet up. She got dressed into something really sexy to show off her curves, and then she was on her way. She arrived at his friend's house and Distance was outside waiting on her. She got out of her car and they hugged as they greeted each other. They both were so happy to see one another, and they embraced while walking inside his friend's house to chill.

While she was sitting down watching a movie that he turned on, he'd constantly look over and just stare at her. She would catch him staring at her, but he would look away each time.

After a few more times, she finally asked him nicely while smiling, "Why do you keep staring at me?"

He looked at her and said, "Because God blessed me."

She was at a loss for words and couldn't say anything but, "Oh, okay."

He then said to her, "Let's go for a ride in my car. You drive."

While they drove, he asked her different questions.

"What do you think about me and you?"

"What do you mean?" she asked.

"What do you think about us being together?"

She said, "I haven't thought about it."

However, in her mind, she had thought about it but was too afraid to tell him how she felt.

He continued, "Well, what if I wanted to be your man?"

She said, "Huh?"

He said, "Huh isn't the answer I was looking for."

She said, "I think we should just be friends."

Secrets knew in her heart that she wanted to be his lady. However, with the circumstances of dealing with her ex, she knew it would cause confusion. She didn't want that drama in this nice man's life. She wanted to tell him that her ex constantly interferes in her love life. Instead, she said nothing, and it made Distance think she wasn't interested in him. In reality, she was crazy about this man.

He simply said, "Oh okay," and left it at that.

They continued to drive. When they arrived at their destination, they parked and got out of the car without further discussion of their budding relationship. They talked about all types of things. It felt like they had known each other forever as they learned more and more about one another. Suddenly, a shooting star went across the sky.

They both saw it, and said, "Wow," before continuing their conversation. It didn't really mean too much to Distance, but to Secrets, it meant so much more. She knew she had met her one true love. There would be a few more shooting stars they both would see on several other occasions while hanging out together. Secrets paid attention to it every time. That night as they returned back to his friend's house, they both talked some more until they got tired, and then she went home.

He said to her, "I'm going to call you when I get home."

She waited for his call and it didn't take long for him to keep his word. They talked nonstop on the phone; neither one wanted to hang up that night. Time passed and they continued to hang out. This time he came to pick her up, and they went riding in his car again. They didn't do anything fancy. It was just something simple to allow them to enjoy each other's presence. Sex was never the topic; they didn't even kiss. They simply enjoyed great conversations and a good time that lasted until the morning.

Chapter
Three

When Distance finally took Secrets home, once again he told her that he would call, and he did just that. However, it didn't go as smoothly as the last time. This time Rhythm popped up at her house. He pretended that he was coming to see their kid, but he had a different agenda. After hearing her on the phone, he reached over and snatched it out of her hand. He began to tell Distance that he and Secrets were in a relationship. Secrets grabbed the phone angrily!

"No, we're not in a relationship anymore!" she told Distance. "Leave my house, Rhythm!"

She was upset that he was there causing problems.

She told him, "You're only here to see our child. Why are you in my business? You need to leave now."

Distance was still on the phone, and Secrets tried explaining. But Distance wasn't trying to hear that.

He said, "I'm going to back off and let you handle your business."

He did just that - he backed off. Secrets was very angry at Rhythm for ruining things. On the contrary, they didn't stay ruined for long because she wasn't about to let Distance go that easily. And little did she know Distance wasn't giving up that easy either.

A few weeks had gone by without any communication between the two of them. They only saw each other at work, but nothing else on a private personal level. They both missed each other and couldn't stay apart anymore. He called her one night talking about some things that happened at work. She hinted around about an event that she was attending with some friends. He said he was going to that same event, so she

told him to save her a dance. He
laughed it off and said that he would,
and then told her he would talk to her
later. The night of the event, he spotted
her and asked her to dance. That led to
them hanging out again. Unfortunately,
Rhythm knew where Secrets would go
out to with her friends, so he would go
to the same club hoping to see her and
Distance together. Secrets was unaware
that Rhythm would even be there on
any night.

One night, he saw them both
together and tried to confront Distance.
Secrets didn't like drama. She was
embarrassed by his actions and tried to
make Rhythm leave her alone. Distance
usually stayed out of it, but that night
he got Rhythm straight and told him
that he didn't want any problems with
him. However, he needed to leave
Secrets alone. Rhythm didn't want any
drama, so he just backed off. Secrets was
relieved. It was as if a burden had been
lifted from her shoulders.

Secrets and Distance continued to get to know each other and became good friends. A few months had gone by, and Secrets' birthday was slowly approaching. She booked a hotel suite to have some private time to enjoy her birthday with her new love Distance. She invited him to her suite, and they had a blast with each other. They enjoyed their time together. As the evening winded down, they decided to take a drive.

They hit the road driving to a nearby city. It was about 45 minutes away, which gave them plenty of time to talk more and be alone together longer. They got some food and gas, and then they turned around and headed back to the suite. While they were driving, Distance asked Secrets once again about them being together. She still wouldn't be honest about how she felt for him.

So she said to him, "I think we're good friends."

He said, "Well, there's a woman that works with us that's interested in me."

Secrets asked him, "Who is she?"

"Don't worry about that," he replied. "Just know she is trying to talk to me."

Secrets said, "Well, why are you telling me this?"

He said, "I just wanted you to know. Besides, you said you're not trying to be with me anyway, right?"

"Nope," she lied.

"Oh okay. Well, from now on, we will just be friends."

They dropped the subject and kept driving back to the suite. When they returned, they sat and talked for the rest of the night. No sex was involved - no kissing or anything. They just enjoyed intimacy. That was until Rhythm called her phone lying that their child wanted to see her, and he was on his way to the suite. Secrets knew he was using their kid just to come where she was. He also wanted to seize the opportunity to be in her business once again. However, for her child's sake, she told him to come.

She gave him the address to the suite, but then she had to get rid of Distance. She knew in her heart that she didn't want him to leave, but she didn't want a physical altercation between him and her ex. Without any other option, Secrets told Distance to leave. That made him very upset. She tried to explain her reasoning, but Distance didn't want to hear it. He felt let down once again, and he was over it. He was done with her.

Secrets felt so bad that she made Distance leave. It really broke her heart to push him away. Shortly after he left, Rhythm showed up and brought her child to her. He was trying to stay and that pissed her off. She told him to leave and to get away from her. It was over. She was completely done with him.

"You're ruining everything for me! Just stay out of my way. If it isn't about our child, then we have nothing else to talk about," she shouted.

Rhythm got upset at her words. As he was leaving, he started to think of all the things he had put her through over the years. He saw how upset she was at him. This time he finally realized that it was over between them, and it was best for him to just move on with his life. Secrets was once really in love with Rhythm. He wasn't a bad person; he just cheated on her a lot. She just got tired of it and didn't want him anymore. She wanted him to let go of trying to win her back because she was over him. However, she did want to remain friends.

Rather than waste the rest of her evening Secrets enjoyed the rest of her birthday at the suite with her child. She put all that drama behind her and made the most of the rest of her evening. She opted to give Distance some space for now. Still, she had unfinished business with him. She didn't like how things turned out between them. She would address those issues in due time.

Part II:

Can We Talk?

Chapter Four

Secrets called Distance several times to explain what happened the night of her birthday, but he wouldn't answer the phone. He was still upset, and she understood why. Several days and missed calls later, Distance eventually talked things over with her. Surprisingly, they were like best friends all over again. He forgave her and dropped his ill feelings about the situation. There was one thing though. He had a new leading lady in his life, which made things very difficult for them.

Secrets felt cheated like her chances of being with her true love had vanished. She wasn't giving up that easy. She also started to wonder if she had helped push him into this other woman's arms with all the space that she was putting between herself and him. Although she was trying to open up to him, the constant interference from Rhythm made that pretty impossible. Nevertheless, she wasn't going to let that stop her.

Even though he was in a new relationship, Distance would still call her from time to time. They were inseparable no matter who or what came between them. They always would manage to find each other. Meanwhile, Secrets kept all her feelings inside and acted like everything was okay when it wasn't. Distance continued on with his new lady. As they got closer, the relationship would be up and down with them. He still always remained close to Secrets.

He would confide in her about his troubled relationship with his new lady. Secrets always told him positive things to build him up. She never used his troubled situation for her gain. She knew that in time her chance to be with him would come again. She believed he was her true love. Still, she told him to try to work things out with his new lady. She also told him not to keep calling her, because she didn't want to be in the middle of their problems.

A few years went by and Secrets left the job where they both worked to work someplace else. She had another child by then… with Rhythm. She wasn't trying to have sex with him, but Rhythm took advantage of her on a drunken night. After finding out she was pregnant, she made it perfectly clear to him that they still weren't getting back together. She was going to have her child, but they would not have any kind of romantic relationship with each other. She felt Rhythm was trying to trap her into being with him, but she wasn't falling for that trick. In the meantime, Distance found out about her having another child. He called her one day to get confirmation.

"Hey, what's this I hear you got a child on the way with Rhythm? I thought you weren't dealing with him anymore."

"No, I wasn't, but he took advantage of me because I was drunk."

"Oh, he's wrong for doing that," Distance replied.

"Yeah, I hear you got a child on the way also."

He replied dryly, "Yeah I do."

The tone of his voice was like he wasn't too thrilled. Secret's felt like he was more concerned about her, and never mentioned also having another kid until she brought it up. But she just kept talking to him like they had done plenty of times before. It was like they had never lost touch from each other. After their phone conversation, she ended up deleting his number just to distance herself from him because she wasn't in a good place at the time and felt alone. After a few months went by she had her child. A little while later, she went back to work.

That following year her birthday was approaching, and she wondered should she call Distance or not. She was hoping maybe he would remember her birthday and they could just talk and see if any feelings were still there between them. She didn't know why, but she felt she needed to talk with him. So she called her old job where he was still working and left a message with his department. She left only her first name and her number for him to call. She didn't know what to expect, but she wanted to see if he would call. To her surprise, he did call her back the same day from work.

"Hey!" he said, sounding so excited to hear from her." "Let me call you back from my cell phone."

After he called from his cell phone, she made sure she kept his number and not delete it as she did before. They talked every day that week and spent time on the phone catching up on old times. That Friday, Secrets was getting her driver's license renewal and bumped into him. They hadn't seen each other in over a year. They'd only talked over the phone.

Distance noticed her first and shouted out her name. "Secrets!"

She turned around and was so happy to see him. She was surprised because she wasn't expecting to see him there. There they were back reunited and they both just so happened to be in the same place at the same time. But only for a split moment... She had no idea that he was about to make a change in their friendship that would tear her heart apart.

He asked, "Is that your new child?"

"Yes," she replied.

"Your child looks just like you. My new child is over there."

She looked in the direction he was pointing and noticed that his lady was sitting across from where they were standing. She was holding their kid and smiling in their direction. Secrets could see his lady seemed very happy, and she would eventually figure out why.

It was later that evening when Distance called. They kept talking about old times, but Secrets couldn't help but wonder how serious his relationship was with his new lady. She knew they always had issues that he often discussed with her. However, this time he never mentioned anything about his relationship. He just kept asking about her life. They eventually ended their conversation for the night.

Later on that night, Secrets was talking to Rhythm. For some reason, it was like every time she was involved with anyone, he would always appear and cause problems. As she continued her conversation with him, her cell phone began to ring. It was Distance calling constantly, but she wouldn't answer. Then, he started to call her home phone. By then, she knew he must have really wanted something, so she answered. Distance said, "Hey! What are you doing? I need to talk to you."

She said, "I'm talking to Rhythm right now, so let me call you back."

Distance really wanted to talk to her right then, but instead, he told her, "Okay. Don't worry about it. Just finish talking to your ex. You have a nice night, and I'll just talk to you later."

Secrets hung up her phone without further conversation. She thought she would just call him later, and he would be there waiting on her like plenty of times before. But not this time. Distance had made his decision, and she'd soon find out what it was when they would speak again. As Secrets was getting ready for work the next morning, she remembered that she told Distance she would call him back. She quickly dialed his number. He answered on the first ring.

She said, "Hey, sorry about last night."

He said, "Oh, that's okay. It doesn't matter now."

Secrets said, "What did you want to talk about?"

He told her, "It doesn't matter now. But I need to finish ironing my clothes so I can walk down this aisle."

"What aisle? Who's getting married?"

"I am," he replied.

At that very moment, her heart fell through the floor.

"No! Don't marry her! She is not the one for you. I love you! Please don't marry her. I have been crazy about you since the day I met you. I didn't want to tell you how I felt. I was so afraid to show my affection for you, and I didn't want to be hurt again," she yelled.

Distance said, "Why are you telling me this now? It's too late."

Secrets cried and poured her heart out.

He said, "Everyone keeps telling me not to marry her, but it's too late now."

"Where are you getting married?" she asked.

"You know I can't tell you that."

"Why didn't you say something earlier? We talked for a whole week, and you didn't mention a word of this."

He replied, "I didn't know how to tell you."

She stopped crying long enough to wish him the best. She didn't want to be bitter about it. A real friend would give well wishes regardless, especially when they truly care. She let him go and they ended their friendship… so they thought. Their relationship was about to take a turn that neither of them ever expected to happen. Things were about to get real.

Sherry D. Lewis

Part III:

When Love Goes Wrong

Chapter Five

Before the wedding bells sounded, Distance realized he was making a huge mistake getting married. His fiancée felt the same way, so they both decided to call off the wedding. They wanted to rethink their lives and not rush into a marriage. This was a relief for Distance, and he quickly called Secrets eager to see how she would react when she found out he didn't get married. He told her that he'd never meant to hurt her. He only was marrying this lady because he had his child and he felt pressured to get married.

Secrets really didn't care for the excuses, but she listened anyway. She told him that she understood why he made the decision to get married and left it at that. The conversation continued and Distance asked to come over because he wanted to see her. She was all for it because she missed him and really wanted to see him, too. She invited him over to her place instead.

When he arrived, they greeted each other with a hug. However, this time the hug was so intense. They could feel the passion thriving between them both. As she went to walk away and allow him to completely enter her home, he reached out and pulled her back into his arms. He squeezed and kissed her so passionately. She couldn't resist because her body was longing for his touch. They had never been intimate sexually throughout the years they had known each other. So this night was long overdue.

He slowly removed her clothes and locked his eyes on her body as if it was the most beautiful picture he'd ever seen. Then, she laid down on her bed as he took off his clothes. Her love moistened at the sight of his naked body. They made love as if they were the last two people on Earth. As their bodies intertwined, their hearts were pounding from excitement.

The sweet taste of sweat dripped from their faces as they fell deeper for each other. There was nothing but hardcore loving all night long as they fulfilled their desire from within. They were both sexual beings, so they pleased each other in every way they could imagine and made that night one to remember. Once they'd finally reached their final climax of the night, they laid with their legs and arms wrapped around each other while gazing into each other's eyes.

They were speechless but very happy that it was what they both anticipated it to be. Thoughts went through their minds. Could this be lust or love? They weren't proud of what just happened considering the circumstances, but it didn't matter because it was what they both wanted and needed.

After that night, they both started to feel they'd made a mistake and needed to end their rendezvous. Yet, it was too late. They were hooked. They started to sneak around every chance they got. Distance would leave his job in the middle of the night just to see Secrets. They would make love all night long until dawn. Then, he would go home to his girlfriend, pretending he had worked all night.

Secrets would plan her whole schedule to make time to be with Distance. Sneaking around wasn't something either one of them was looking forward to doing, but it continued constantly for a few months until jealousy and rage came into play. Secrets wanted to see other people, and Distance was not having it. However, she wasn't going to put her life on hold waiting for him. He was still in a relationship with another woman, and Secrets wanted out of the romance. Distance wasn't too thrilled. Although he also wanted to end the romance, he

Sherry D. Lewis

didn't want Secrets with another man.

He got jealous and would sit out in her yard waiting for her to get home. Secrets was still so in love with him. Therefore, she would fall right into his arms and make passionate love every time they got together. However, one night Distance called and wanted to see Secrets, but she had company with another man. That made him very angry. He knew he couldn't say much because he had a woman of his own. That didn't stop him from wanting to control her social life. He would tell Secrets not to hang out at clubs with her friends. He felt it would bring attention from other men.

He knew he didn't have any right to tell Secrets how to live her life, but he tried anyway. When they did get together, she would sometimes go through his phone and see naked pictures of other women. She'd also read the messages they would leave for him. She knew it was wrong to invade his privacy, but they were both being foolish and immature. When she would confront him, Distance would explain that the women didn't mean anything to him. He claimed the communication with them was only for attention that he wasn't receiving from her or at home. Secrets would tell him that he was full of it and that she didn't believe anything he had to say.

This romance turned very toxic. They would argue constantly. They were often yelling and screaming over the phone at each other. Things got very tense between them, and they knew what needed to be done. So they talked things over and made one final decision to end their romance. Especially while nobody knew of it but them. The romance just wasn't good for them. However, they remained good friends. Then, things would turn for the worst for Distance, and a friend is what he was going to need the most.

Chapter Six

Distance lost his job and fell on hard times. His girlfriend didn't want to support him because she was only with him for his money. She took her kid and left him. He told Secrets that although his girlfriend never knew of his other romance, he felt bad and that it was all his fault. Secrets told him not to feel bad about losing a job because things happen. Distance started to realize she was right. He also later found out that his girlfriend was cheating on him. Right then, he was even more convinced that getting married would've been a mistake.

As time passed, Distance picked up the pieces and moved on with his life. He found another job and got his own place. He even started dating other women and really living the single life. He became a real lady's man, and his friends made sure his place was the ultimate bachelor's pad. Secrets wasn't too thrilled about the other women, but she just played her part and tried not to think about it. Besides, they weren't in a relationship. Therefore, she couldn't say much anyway.

One day, Distance called Secrets to come over to chill at his new place. She was at work but agreed to come right after her shift ended. When Secrets got home from work, she showered and changed into something sexier. They weren't a couple, but they still were close friends that had a lot of sex. When she was ready to visit, she called Distance. However, his phone would go straight to voicemail.

She didn't want to keep calling back to back, so she spaced the calls out. He knew when she got off work, so it was strange that he wasn't answering her calls. She thought maybe it slipped his mind. Nevertheless, she waited a

few minutes and called again. This time
his phone rang, and another woman
answered. It made Secrets very angry,
so she went to his place to confront him.
She'd had enough of the disrespect and
other women. She'd played her part
long enough.

Distance could be very controlling
and very selfish at times. He wanted his
cake and wanted to eat it, too. Secrets
wasn't having that this time. She pulled
into his residence, got out her car, and
knocked at his door. A woman opened
the door half-naked, and Distance was
standing behind her drunk and talking
crazy. Secrets didn't say anything to the
woman because she never would
confront a woman over a man.
However, she did have a few words for
Distance.

"Look, I don't appreciate being
stood up or being played. You got me
messed up! I don't want shit else to do
with you!"

Distance got mad and slammed
his door in her face. But Secrets wasn't

done. She started showing her ass. She got so angry that she started cursing loudly at him. Distance stormed out the door telling her to leave. Instead of getting into her car, she grabbed a baseball bat from the passenger seat and ran towards him with it. She started swinging at him. He tried to grab her to calm her down, but she hit his wrist by mistake and broke his watch. His hand immediately began to swell. Distance made the other woman leave so he could calm things down with Secrets.

Secrets started to calm down and Distance tried to explain why he never called. He even apologized for standing her up. This calmed her even more, so they left his place and went back to her apartment where they talked things over. They tried to be more respectful of each other. Through all that drama, he didn't call the police on her. Distance didn't want to see her in any trouble. Therefore, he decided to put that night behind him and move forward with their non-relationship but mutual feelings.

One late night, they were enjoying each other's company at her place. They decided to go to the store around the corner from her apartments. They drove Distance's car and ended up in a fender bender. A guy had run the red light and hit their car. The cops came out and got the reports on each vehicle in the accident. The other person's vehicle was towed due to no insurance. However, for Distance and Secrets, things would take a different route. They waited and wondered what was taking the officer so long. Distance's vehicle had car insurance, so that wasn't the issue.

Finally, the officer walked over to them and told Distance that he was under arrest for unpaid parking tickets.

Distance started yelling at the officer, "I don't owe anything!"

The officer just placed Distance into the patrol car and walked backed towards Secrets.

"You're also under arrest for unpaid parking tickets."

Meanwhile, another officer came to the scene. He placed her into the second patrol car. She could hear yelling and screaming through the window at the officer.

"Let her go! Why are you arresting her?!"

Neither Distance nor Secrets could believe what was happening. He was angry and she was terrified. However, after a few hours, they bonded out of jail and took care of everything to clear their record. Once they were home, they both laughed at each other. They weren't laughing about the unpaid tickets. They just thought it was funny that they were arrested together. Through that whole process, they both took the time to re-evaluate the people they had been seeing. In their time of need, they tried calling everyone, and none of their friends came to rescue either one of them from jail. Their families were the only ones that helped them.

Both Secrets and Distance started
to see that none of their friends really
had their backs as they did for each
other. As a result, they decided that they
would move in together when each of
their apartment leases ended. They also
agreed that they would always be down
for each other. They'd soon learn that
sometimes you don't really know what
it's like being with a person until you
live with them. Things would occur
that would challenge their friendship. It
all wasn't as bad as it seemed. Although
they would have struggles and financial
burdens, the love and respect they
shared for each other would keep them
together.

Chapter
Seven

As planned, they moved in together and things got pretty interesting. Distance would often drink heavily. One day, he even went to work late because he had too much to drink the night before. His manager got tired of the tardiness and fired him. To combat the depression of losing his job, he started drinking heavier and heavier. He cared about nothing but alcohol. He would look for work but would constantly get turned down. No matter what he tried to do, no one would hire him.

Distance got very depressed and lost faith. And he gave up on himself. People would talk about him, calling him lazy and treating him like a nobody. They would constantly tell

Secrets to leave him because he had no job and nothing to offer her. However, she stayed down for him. She was a real chick that was down for her best friend - this man that she really loved. They lived together for four long years with only her working.

During this time, she had to pay all the bills by herself, which made things very stressful for her. She would continue to motivate him and encourage him to not give up on life. She did everything she could to make him see that things would get better for him. But all along she was screaming inside for help of any kind. Secrets wanted to be rescued from the financial burden that was placed upon her. Distance started praying more and restoring his faith. Suddenly, life got better for him. He found another job and got back on his feet. He would begin to see things differently and look at life more seriously. He started to realize the importance of doing what's right.

With the fresh start, Distance changed his life for the better. He never was a bad person, but he was lost spiritually. He got closer to God and asked for forgiveness for all his sins. Then, he began to live his life for Jesus. He became happier with his life, more than he had ever imagined. On the contrary, it would take Secrets a little bit longer to seek her full potential. There was a different assignment for her life. She still needed to go through something for her to be free. She suffered from a lot of mental and emotional depression that she hid from Distance and everyone for years. She was a strong-willed woman, but she faced a lot of difficult mental challenges. Sometimes we don't realize that just because a person is always being strong doesn't mean they don't have weak moments.

A bond that once was so close between them started to feel so far away. They both had gotten so far away from their true selves that they didn't remember what went wrong in their relationship. Secrets went into a depression, and Distance would try to help her the same as she did for him. However, she didn't feel like she needed help. Eventually, the mental turmoil took a toll on her. She would act out in anger and violence when something made her mad. Her anger would go from zero to one thousand in minutes. Then, it would take about an hour before she would calm down.

She would argue constantly at Distance. She would even rip up his clothes and fight him. He would try his best to restrain her, and he never would fight her back. She would embarrass him in front of his friends by doing everything she could to physically and verbally hurt him. She would take all his clothes and throw them on the streets because she was mad that he didn't cook any dinner. She would change the door locks if he stayed out too late. He'd be forced to sleep in his car because she wouldn't let him into the house. She even hit him in the head one time with a hammer. She was standing in the driveway trying to leave to go to a party. Distance wanted her to stay home with him, but she felt controlled. So she went to the washroom and grabbed a hammer. She started swinging it around and around towards Distance and mistakenly hit him.

She never really wanted to hurt him. She just wanted to scare him. Instead, it scared her. When she saw blood, she thought she hurt him badly. Thank God. it was just a scratch. After that, she stopped picking up anything to swing towards him. Still, deep inside she was hurting. She knew in her heart that she was wrong, and she would always apologize. Nonetheless, the damage was done, and apologizing doesn't change anything. Despite the bad days, Distance loved this woman, and he still stayed with her. His friend thought he was crazy, and even Secrets thought he was crazy for staying with her. But he loved her through her pain. Because he felt love would always win over anything.

Chapter Eight

The relationship got worse and Distance couldn't take anymore. He decided to leave the relationship and move out. He didn't want to leave but Secrets made their life together so uncomfortable for him that he had to leave. She told him she didn't want him living with her anymore and leaving would be best. So, that's exactly what he did. He moved out and got his own place. After Distance left, Secrets realized just how much she needed him. She didn't need him for finance or sex. She needed him for companionship. Secrets felt safe and whole around Distance. Now that he had moved out, she felt alone.

Secrets had blamed Distance for everything she was going through but never looked at herself. She started to realize just how lost she was and how much pain she caused herself and Distance. She began to change her life for the better. She started to pour her time into spiritual healing. She even sought advice for mental health. As she got stronger mentally, she became wiser. Secrets gained a piece of mind and was happier than she thought she could ever be.

It took some time, but she and Distance began to rekindle their relationship - but only as friends and not lovers. Secrets was so grateful for Distance leaving her because it helped her become a better woman. Being apart for so long helped them realize just how much love they had for each other. No matter who they met, it never put a wedge between them. Years went by, and things started to get better in their relationship. It was almost like it was when they first met.

Distance would have other relationships, that would make him fall head over heels. He would always treat these ladies like queens. Yet, not everybody is meant to be on a royal court. They may appear to be honest and loyal, but most of the time they're just playing the part.

All the ladies that Distance dated knew they had found a good man and didn't want to let him go. One lady, in particular, was determined to be with him. Secrets always warned him about her because she could always sense the lady was up to no good. He just brushed it off and paid Secrets no attention. He assumed it was jealousy, but she'd never been the jealous type. She could just sense something just wasn't right with this woman.

Distance and his new lady would go through problems, but he never wanted to tell Secrets about it. He knew she was right all along but didn't know what to say. It turns out the lady was a con-artist. She was living a double life with another man. Distance found out about it through a mutual friend that knew of the guy she was living with, and it crushed his heart into a thousand pieces. He was actually falling for this woman, but she let him down.

He soon realized that all his jewelry and even money that he had saved had disappeared. He would eventually tell Secrets about his misfortune. It was overwhelming for him, and he needed to tell someone he trusted about what was happening. Secrets wasn't too surprised, because she had her doubts about the other woman all along. She just didn't want to say, "I told you so" to his face. Instead, she just listened and comforted him in his time of need. Being a friend as always.

Secrets eventually told Distance he needed to slow down with all these women, and try being alone, and just love yourself better. And allow love to come to him. Because if it found him once, it will find him again. Distance took her advice and ended all communication with his lady. He asked her to move out, and then he used his alone time to find himself again. He traveled the world and left all things in his past behind him. He even left Secrets behind.

Distance would write letters to keep in touch with her. However, that was all the communication they shared. It started to become a very long "distance" relationship. Though it seemed they were growing apart, love was still in their hearts. Distance seemed to be doing fine. On the other hand, Secrets started to regret telling him to live alone. She began to feel abandoned. It was as if he'd left her behind with everything and everybody else. Rather than waste time having a pity party, Secrets stopped dating and took her own advice. She stayed alone without knowing that she needed a break herself. Surprisingly, love would find her again when she least expected it.

Chapter Nine

Secret no longer had any distractions from Distance or any other male friends. She finished her classes and earned her degree. When she was dating, she'd forgotten about her goals and was not fulfilling her purpose in life. Her freedom and self-focus allowed her to see what she needed to do for herself. She became very successful and lived the life she always dreamed of living. Meanwhile, she met a handsome guy that was about to turn her world of being alone into being married.

This man was absolutely dreamy, and Secrets was totally caught off guard. No other man had ever measured up to Distance. However, this guy was all that and some. She had spent so many years focusing on herself and her career that she had forgotten about romance and love. Therefore, she didn't see this one coming.

One evening, she was out with a few coworkers for a business meeting. They decided to go out for drinks afterward. While she was enjoying her evening, a guy approached her and told her that she was absolutely the most beautiful woman he had ever seen. Secrets told herself that this man was just telling her anything so he could sleep with her. Yet, as the conversation continued, she thought of something to see just how interested he was in her. She told him she was laid off from her job and was about to be evicted from her home. She also said that she had to raise her two children alone.

The guy told her that he understood that things happen. Still, if she is interested, he wanted to take her out and maybe take her mind off her problems. Secrets smiled a little and agreed. With that, they officially introduced themselves to each other. He told her that his name was Pretender.

Then, they exchanged numbers and made plans to meet again. As time passed, they would talk and go out on dates. The two of them got along really well.

After months of getting to know Pretender, Secrets felt bad for lying about being laid off and being on the verge of getting evicted. She eventually told him the truth, and they just laughed about it. He told her that he understood and that he enjoyed the little mystery game she played on him. This guy was so charming with his dashing good looks. His charm coupled with his good looks made him so irresistible. But Secrets was no fool. She always remembered that nothing is perfect, and everything that glitters isn't always gold.

After a long exciting time of dating, a person from her past would soon interrupt this new romance that was trying to bloom. Nevertheless, Secrets and her new beau started to get very acquainted with each other. Their budding relationship was actually going great. It was better than she expected. Two years had gone by before they knew it.

One day she was getting ready for a birthday celebration for her man Pretender. He turned his special day even more special and proposed to her. She said yes but secretly she never stopped thinking about Distance. She always thought of him. She would try to block out her feelings for him, but they would still be there calling out for him. Secrets and her new man Pretender began a life together, except they weren't married yet. They both lived separately because Secrets didn't want to live together until they tied the knot.

One day as their wedding was approaching, she received a letter in the mail. The letter was from Distance. He was writing to inform her that he was moving back home, and he had something important to talk about with her. They couldn't wait to catch up on everything with one another. As planned, Distance arrived back home. Before he could even get settled in, he called Secrets. What he didn't know was that she wasn't the same available woman that she was when he left years ago. Furthermore, Secrets wasn't really ready to tell Distance about her new love and her new life.

After several attempts to call Secrets, they finally got the chance to catch up on old times and talk about all the new things that had happened in their lives over the years. Still, Secrets never mentioned her man – better yet, her fiancé. She remained quiet on the topic of their love lives. Distance noticed but assumed maybe it was because they hadn't seen each other in so long and that things had changed so much between them. In reality, Secrets wasn't talking because she was thinking of the right moment and words to say. She needed the words to tell her best friend and love of her life that she was engaged to be married.

By now, her wedding was in a few days, and she still didn't mention anything to Distance. It made her realize why he never mentioned his wedding to her years ago. It's difficult telling somebody you have strong feelings for them when you're getting married. You have so many emotions running that you can become very nervous.

As the night went on, Secrets' phone rang off the hook… with her man on the other end. He would call constantly, but she ignored his calls. After her lovely conversation with Distance was over, she called Pretender back and told him that her phone had been misplaced. She told him that she saw the missed calls when she found it. He was so understanding and didn't think twice about it. She felt bad about lying, but the truth would have hurt him more.

As the wedding date slowly approached, Distance and Secrets continued to catch up. They would talk on the phone for hours. He would share with her about all his adventures and how he's doing financially great for himself. Both of their children had grown up and were all doing well, also. They congratulated each other on their accomplishments and becoming wiser and better people. They finished up their conversation and ended the call.

Pretender had to travel out of town for business, but he would return just in time for their wedding. While he was away, Secrets and Distance would spend more time talking on the phone to each other. She finally felt it was time to tell him about her new man and engagement. Distance called to meet up with her. They met at their favorite restaurant. Secrets was already there at the restaurant sitting in her car when Distance arrived. Seeing him after so many years made her heart melt all over again. They greeted each other with a passionate hug and then went inside. The more they enjoyed each other that evening, the more they remembered why they fell in love in the first place.

They shared remarkable chemistry like no other.

"I have something important to tell… well… ask you," Distance told Secrets."

Her heart melted instantly as she sat there gazing into his eyes. Then he popped the question.

"Will you marry me?" he asked.

Secrets wasn't even expecting her first proposal. So to have two proposals was just over the top for her. She just sat there speechless. Distance was puzzled. He needed to know why she wasn't saying yes and being a little more excited. She finally found her words.

"Um, I have to go. I have an important meeting for work the next day."

Without another word, she got up from her chair and left. Distance just stayed there at the restaurant with a perplexed look, wondering what had just happened. However, soon, lots more was about to happen.

Part IV:

When Love is Actually Real Love

Chapter Ten

The next day Distance called Secrets to get her answer to his proposal. However, she never answered her phone. Seeing him calling made her very nervous. In her heart, she wanted more than anything to say yes. Still, she knew that she had to make up her mind and choose wisely on who she should marry. Meanwhile, Pretender returned, and they picked up right where they left off. She didn't feel comfortable having a secret hidden from him, so she told him about Distance. He was shocked but didn't worry because he was confident in himself and knew that Distance didn't stand a chance against him.

Secrets called Distance and explained why she left the night before. She informed him about her engagement and that the wedding was happening in a few days. Distance didn't get upset. He just congratulated her. Even though she still hadn't given him an answer, he knew that he didn't need one. Especially not after she left with no explanation the night before. He assumed she'd already chosen who she wanted. He just hung up the phone and never called her back.

When the wedding day came, Secrets couldn't be any happier and clearer on what she needed to do. However, as she prepared to walk down the aisle, everything she could think of went wrong. She was really hoping Distance would crash the wedding and take her into his arms, but that wasn't going to happen. On the contrary, what did happen was that her wedding finally got on track. Everything went as planned with no distractions.

Finally, she got ready to put on her dress when a gut feeling came over her. It was then that she realized that she was making a huge mistake marrying Pretender. She knew it wasn't going to be pretty, but she called the wedding off within minutes of saying, "I do."

Her man, now soon-to-be-ex, was devastated. Secrets didn't want to hurt him, but it actually was for the better. To add to the drama, he flipped the script on her and said she wasn't really who he wanted. In fact, he was just getting married for financial gain. He only wanted to make his business strive further. Secrets didn't care about anything he was saying. She was just relieved that she didn't hurt herself by being in a marriage that wasn't going to be based on love. Instead, it would only be based on business.

After the wedding was called off, Secrets got on with her life and got back to herself. She still hadn't talked to Distance. Every day she thought about him and wondered what he was doing. She tried to call, but he never answered or returned her calls. Once again, she started to regret letting him get away. Months had gone by, and still, there was no communication from Distance. Secrets started to give up on being with him. She felt hopeless and didn't know if Distance had given up on her. He wasn't communicating with her at all, and she was sure that she had lost her chance to be with him. She was afraid her love would be lost forever.

As Secrets sat thinking about Distance, she started to reminisce about all the good times they had together. She thought about all the wonderful things he would do to show his love for her. There were so many regrets that she carried around with her for years. She had regrets about not taking a chance on love with the man who stole her heart away years ago when they first met. She felt like maybe she didn't deserve love. Although she'd never wronged anyone she was in a relationship with, she thought romantic relationships just weren't for her.

She felt bad about the romance she had with him when he was already in a relationship. Maybe she was getting karma turned back on her. Nevertheless, days turned into weeks. Weeks turned into months, and months turned into years still with no communication from Distance. She knew he was working and still had his own place. She even knew how to find him, but she wasn't going to bother him. It tore her up inside not being able to see or hear from the love of her life. She knew she had screwed up and was beating herself up over it.

To cope, she just poured herself into her work and let her love life take a backseat once and for all. But who was she fooling? Maybe she was fooling herself because she needed to see him to ease her mind. So she called him to talk, and he actually answered the phone. But Distance said he didn't want anything to do with her. He told her they could be friends but nothing else. Secrets was heartbroken that Distance was acting so mean towards her. She didn't want to lose him again, but Distance was over it.

Secrets respected his wishes and just walked away knowing in her heart she loved this man more than any other man she'd ever dated. Sadly, she had no other choice but to let him go.

Distance was not quite over the fact that Secrets ran out on him after his proposal to her. She left him with no clue to what her answer would be, and she even left out the fact that she was already engaged. Marriage was far from his mind now. Distance was all about being single and not being tied down. Secrets decided to put the past behind her and Distance with it. However, she wasn't quite done with her past because her ex-fiancé wasn't ready to be done with her.

Pretender called her to discuss the whole disaster of a wedding they tried to have. He told her he was only saying those things about financial gain just to not look like a fool. He was upset that she was calling the wedding off and ready to leave him at the altar. He told her that she was all he wanted, and he was willing to give her the space she needed to be left alone. Secrets was still upset about Distance. She started feeling depressed again because she needed a man's touch. She desired the comfort of feeling wanted. So she got back with Pretender and things just got out of hand from there.

Secrets started to become insecure with her appearance and her weight. She didn't understand why she kept feeling so down all the time, and Pretender didn't make matters any better. She would constantly catch him on the phone talking to other women, but he would say it was work-related. She wanted to believe him, so she did; however, she kept her eyes and ears wide open. It was hard to keep an eye on him because they still lived in separate houses. Every time she would call him, he would be busy or tired. He never made any quality time for her.

One night she asked to come over to spend time with him because she was lonely. He said okay, but right before she arrived, he texted her to hold off because he needed to go to his office to get something he forgot. Secrets knew it was a lie, but she played right along with his little game. Still, she went to his house anyway, expecting to see another woman. She waited in her car and parked in a corner. She waited and waited but didn't see any signs of anyone being at his home. Yet, her intuition made her feel something was going on inside his home.

As she sat there and continued to think, she got more and more anxious to know if he was cheating. She got out of her car and walked around to his bedroom window to listen for any sounds of him being with another woman. She didn't hear anything, but she still wasn't leaving until she got the answers she sought. She knocked at the door and no one answered. She knocked again, and he finally opened the door.

"What are you doing here? I told you not to come," he said.

"Yeah, you did. Why aren't you at your office?"

"I finished up early and headed back home, but I forgot to call you back," he lied.

"Okay… Are you gonna let me in?"

And as she tried to walk in, he stopped her. What did he do that for? That just made her more anxious to see what he was hiding. He told her to leave and that he was tired. Then, he closed the door in her face. Secrets just stood there thinking of all the drama she went through with Distance, Carrion, and Rhythm. Once again, she felt unappreciated. When you're tired of being unappreciated you don't have any control over your actions. Secrets was not an insane woman. She just needed to get her point across, that she wasn't to be messed with.

So, as she stood outside his door her mind clicked, and all she could see was a fire in her eyes and rage in her heart. She kicked his door in and saw him just sitting alone. She felt so stupid for making a fool of herself. They had many words back and forth. They were screaming and arguing with each other when another woman walked up.

Secrets just looked at Pretender with tears in her eyes. Their relationship was barely back together again. Instead of him trying to get closer to her and trying to build a stronger bond between them, he was cheating on her with several women. She left his home and went back to her house to gather her thoughts. She knew she had messed up. She wasn't sure what would happen that night, but he didn't call the police on her for kicking in his door. However, his neighbors did, and things were looking really bad for her. She was about to lose everything she had worked so hard for all because she was hurt and broken.

Chapter Eleven

The detectives came out to his home the next day to get information on what happened and then get a warrant for her arrest. However, Pretender would need to press charges against her. He didn't want to do that. The detective asked if he was sure? He told him that he was. The detective dropped the charges and left. Pretender called Secrets to let her know the neighbors called the police because she was disturbing the peace. After seeing the door, they added vandalism. He told her that he didn't press charges and the detective also dropped the charges against her.

She was relieved to know that she was in the clear, but it didn't change her mind for revenge. Secrets thought of several things to do to him just to feel better from being cheated on. Still, she knew it was best not to act on any of those thoughts. She decided to take a step back to calm down. A few days later, Pretender called to come to visit her. She let him come over, although he was being unfaithful. She wanted passion and love so badly that she was losing her dignity and self-respect. Accepting this kind of behavior from any man was ridiculous, but she still allowed him to be in her presence.

Pretender never really took the time to notice how unhappy she was. To him, all that mattered was getting his way and doing whatever made him happy.

One day they were out on a dinner date with some of his friends from his job. Looking around at everyone enjoying themselves, Secrets felt she didn't belong and wanted to be anywhere else other than that date. To make matters worse, Pretender didn't pay any attention to her the whole evening. Secrets noticed that he was more attentive to his friends than to her.

She thought back to him saying he only wanted to marry her for financial gain. With all the disrespect, infidelity, and lies, she knew her relationship with him was based on building his career. It definitely wasn't based on love. Meanwhile, the whole time she sat there at that dinner, she thought about nothing but Distance. Yet the heartache of how he treated her when they last talked, made her stop thinking about him very quickly.

As they left the dinner date and headed home, she thought about all her failed relationships. At that very moment, she knew nobody could love her better than she could love herself. She told Pretender they needed to talk. She explained to him how depressed and unhappy she was, and she needed a break from their relationship. She was tired of the whole dating scene. She told him she wanted out of their relationship and wanted to be left alone. He agreed to break up and didn't really get upset. He did apologize for all the cheating though. He also asked if they could remain friends. She agreed.

Secrets was exhausted and needed to search for the love she once had for herself. This time, she was willing to "distance" herself from anything and anyone who didn't mean her any good. She would do whatever it took to find true happiness. Years ago, she brought herself out of a depression, and it worked out. Then, she ended up getting depressed all over again. This time she was determined to face her fears and overcome all the failures and everything that was against her.

It took some time but with a lot of focusing on herself, she was able to get back to being independent. After all the heartbreaks, mental and emotional breakdowns, and allowing other people to take advantage of her kindness, she became a tough woman who knew her self-worth. She became a woman that was going to stand for what she believed in. She wasn't taking less than royalty from anyone. She was determined to make sure depression would never bring her down ever again.

After getting herself together, she was able to focus more on her goals. She was able to build her business to a multi-million dollar company. With all that success, she still wanted to share it with Distance. He was the only one who really believed in her goals other than herself. One thing he always did was encourage her no matter what was going on between them personally. He wanted her to have better and become successful. She wanted to call him, but she didn't want to get disappointed if he didn't want to talk to her. So, she tried very hard to block Distance out of her mind. No matter how much she worked or kept herself occupied, he would still be in her heart no matter what. They were friends first and that's what mattered.

Distance was off living his life. He was trying to keep his mind off Secrets.

He would constantly deny how he felt about her every time anyone asked him about her. He knew she didn't get married because his friends told him. They also let him know she was still single and very successful. His family and friends would encourage him to talk to Secrets and try to reconnect with her. They would tell him if he really loved this woman, then go get her back because true friendships are important. Furthermore, with their history, they shouldn't let go of each other since real friends are hard to find.

Distance spent a lot of time alone in his home. He felt maybe he was better off alone and didn't need anyone in his space. He had been let down so many times before, and this time wasn't any different. He was stubborn, but he also loved very hard and would do anything for anyone - especially the ones he loved. When he found a woman he loved, he made sure she knew exactly how much she was loved. He was so kind and thoughtful. He wouldn't always verbally say, "I love you," but he most definitely showed it. He would express his love to anyone he was dating, but he showed his affection more. To him, actions always spoke louder than words. This is what Secrets loved about him.

These two unique individuals were so similar, that it was just heartbreaking to see them apart. It was sad that they weren't allowing their wonderful spirits to embrace each other with passion and affection. They needed to show sweet kindness to each other. Distance eventually started to check up on Secrets without her even knowing. He wanted to call her, but he was stubborn and didn't want to be let down anymore by her. Still, he was a smart man and knew exactly what to do to meet up with her without actually communicating directly to her.

Every day when he would get off work, he would walk by her job thinking he might bump into her, but it never happened. He thought of so many ways to see her. They both wanted each other, and all they had to do was put their differences aside and just call each other. However, stubbornness was in the way, but fate would prevail.

One day Secrets had to leave work early because she had some issues that prevented her from doing her duties. After she left work, she decided to take a stroll in the park. It was the same park she and Distance walked through years ago. This time she was walking alone and thinking of all the choices she had made. She realized how happy she was for choosing the greatest love of all – and that was by loving herself. She continued to walk and thought about a lot of things that made her happy. After a few more steps, she decided to sit and take a break from walking.

She looked around and was shocked at the sight. Distance was sitting right across from her looking down at his phone. Without any hesitation, she yelled over to him. He looked up and smiled. They both slowly walked towards each other with no expectations of anything happening. Without saying another word, they grabbed each other very passionately and kissed. There was something different about this kiss. It wasn't a normal regular kiss, but it was a *familiar kiss*. It was a kiss that reminded them both why they fell in love in the first place.

This time they had no baggage, no other mates, and no distractions. It was just the two of them being what they were destined to be all along. They were two people who genuinely love each other and found the greatest love ever. They learned to love themselves which made it easier to love someone else without regrets or blaming each other for their mistakes. They didn't need to ask any questions or explain anything. There still was a question that most definitely needed to be answered. However, with the love that they have for each other, it was hard to guess. The on-again and off-again type of romance they shared made it very difficult for them to decide their fate. Still, the question remained: What will be her answer to his proposal? Stay tuned...